Goats For Sale

Written by Dorothy Carbo
Illustrated by Michael Gancarz

Four Directions Press
Rhinebeck New York

Copyright © 2016 Dorothy Carbo.
All rights reserved.

Published in the United States by Four Directions Press,
P. O. Box 417, Rhinebeck, New York, 12572.

ISBN 978-0-9627659-9-5

LIBRARY OF CONGRESS CONTROL NUMBER 2016912715

Printed by CreateSpace, an Amazon.com Company

Published August, 2016
FIRST EDITION

Available from Amazon.com and other book stores

For Linda, who made it happen.

In Farmer Brown's barn
      was a morning surprise.

4 baby goats born
      before his shocked eyes.

Well my goat gives me milk,
      and then I make cheese.

But what will I do
      with all of these?

A neighboring farmer made a suggestion,

"Friend Farmer Brown,
        I'll answer your question.

Wait till they're stronger,
        and fully grown

And sell 'em to folks
        who want a goat of their own."

So one spring day
　　　when the weather was fine,

He made up some letters
　　　and fashioned a sign:

```
G O A T S
  FOR
  SALE
```

And put it on a chair
　　　where folks pick up mail.

He'd forgot, down the road
      lived a mischevous lad,

Who the neighbors blamed
      for everthing bad.

One day a man came
　　　　and knocked on the door.

"I saw your sign on the way to the store.

How much for the oats –
　　　　by the sack or the pound?

Are they whole oats still
　　　　or have they been ground?"

"*Oats?*" said the farmer,
　　　　"I don't grow any oats.

What I have for sale are
　　　　4 baby goats."

"Well come look at your sign.
　　　　I'm not mistaken."

And sure he was right,
　　　　The **G** had been taken.

The farmer went straight
        to the lad by the brook

And chastised him
        to return the letter he took.

The boy laughed
        and said, "It was just a joke,"

And returned the letter,
        but part of it broke.

The farmer had gone back
        to his barn and his chore

And trusted that the boy
        would mischief no more.

But then came the waited-for
        knock on the door.

A man wanted to buy
        what was advertised for.

"Those coats that you're selling –
        are they fur or of cloth?
Are they in good condition
        or been eaten by moth?

What colors and sizes?
        I need large and light.
I'll buy the whole lot,
        if the price is right."

"*Coats* ??? This is a farm,
        not a factory sir.

We don't sell coats –
        not of cloth or of fur.

What we have are 4 goats
        that give milk to make cheese.
If you'd like to see them,
        step this way, please."

"Goats? I live in the city
      in a three-room flat.

There's no goats allowed
      in a house like that."

The boy, who had tried
　　　　to correct a bad deed

That was founded in fun,
　　　　not in hate or in greed,

Had tried to explain:
　　　　he returned letter "**G**"

But the fact that it broke,
　　　　made it look like a "**C**,"

But there's no way to reason
　　　　with an angry old man.

Since the boy got the blame,
　　　　he went on with his plan.

Again the farmer checked his ad

And looked for the boy
        and his jokes that were bad.

When he scolded the boy
        and made loud angry threats,

Was the day about which
        he still has regrets.

One day he replaced the "**G**"
with a "**B**,"

And boats were requested
though far from the sea.

Moats were offered,
             but that went too far,

'cause how do you tie them
             on top of your car?

He lost the "**G**,"
    but still played the game.

With fewer letters,
    the fun was the same.

One day, baseball teams sought
to buy the man's bats.

An animal shelter came
to rescue his cats.

A collector of headgear
wanted all of his hats.

A houseware store
made an offer on mats.

One day, while deciding
　　　　a new farmer's ware,

He left just the sign

```
┌─────────────────┐
│                 │
│      F O R      │
│      S A L E    │
│                 │
└─────────────────┘
```

on the chair.

Then came antique dealers
　　　　and homemakers who

Fought over that chair;
　　　　they would've bought two.

The game went on till
fall chilled the air.

The farmer was feeling
a sense of despair.

After the summer
the buyers are few,

So he had to figure out
something else to do.

"I'll keep all my goats;

From their milk I'll make cheese.

I wonder if that's a good product
to freeze."

He became known for his goat cheese
in the whole countryside,

And people came to buy from far and wide.

The nanny was happy
she kept every kid.

The boy realized
the mischief he did.

The farmer got rich filling
cheese orders by mail,

And never put up his…

The End

Dorothy Carbo
Author

Dorothy Carbo (née Zullo) is now an octogenarian. She was born in Brooklyn, moved up the Hudson River to Kingston, spent many years in Schenectady with relatives, and now resides in Dutchess County, New York — all in all, a true New Yorker.

She holds a bachelor's degree in Education from Hunter and Brooklyn Colleges, and a master's degree in Counseling Psychology from Long Island University.

She has previously published *A Fixit Guide For Women* as a home repair specialist and advocate for women's capabilities.

She has a penchant for rhyme and fun. "These stories were written many years ago for my children Linda, Patricia, and Joseph, my niece and nephew Patty and Michael, and my grandchildren Noah and Zachary, and whenever my muse Erato would deign to visit," she says.

She hopes you enjoy her stories as much as she enjoys writing them for you. She continues to write as a member of the Society of Children's Book Writers & Illustrators.

Michael Gancarz
Illustrator

Michael Gancarz received his Bachelor of Fine Arts degree from the State University of New York at New Paltz. Two of his paintings are part of the permanent collection at Mount Saint Mary College Gallery in Newburg, New York. His work has been published in *Stretching Canvas* magazine and *Loburn* magazine. He currently works with the developmentally disabled.

34245599R00025

Made in the USA
Middletown, DE
13 August 2016